D0575055

Robert D. San Souci

The Hobyahs

illustrated by Alexi Natchev

A Doubleday Book for Young Readers

TETON COUNTY LIBRARY
JACKSON, WYOMING

A Doubleday Book for Young Readers
Published by
Delacorte Press
Bantam Doubleday Dell Publishing Group, Inc.
1540 Broadway
New York, New York 10036
Doubleday and the portrayal of an anchor with a dolphin are trademarks of
Bantam Doubleday Dell Publishing Group, Inc.

Text copyright © 1994 by Robert D. San Souci
Illustrations copyright © 1994 by Alexi Natchev
All rights reserved. No part of this book may be reproduced or transmitted in
any form or by any means, electronic or mechanical, including photocopying,
recording, or by any information storage and retrieval system, without the
written permission of the Publisher, except where permitted by law.

Library of Congress Cataloging in Publication Data
San Souci, Robert D.
The Hobyahs / Robert D. San Souci ; illustrated by Alexi Natchev.
p.   cm.
Summary: Five faithful dogs save their mistress from the
dreadful Hobyahs.
ISBN 0-385-30934-1
[1. Fairy tales. 2. Folklore—England.] I. Natchev, Alexi, ill. II. Title.
PZ8.S248Ho   1994   398.24'52974442—dc20
[E]   92-28655   CIP   AC

Typography by Lynn Braswell

Manufactured in Italy
April 1994
10 9 8 7 6 5 4 3 2 1
Nil

To Mark, Irene, and Michaela Figari —
with love from
"Cousin Bob" (R.S.S.)

To my friends — there and here.
A.N.

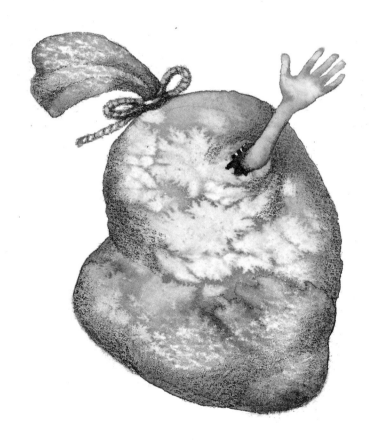

ED. 11/19/94 14.95

By moonlight and by starlight,
Within the forest deep,
The Hobyahs plot their mischief,
While good folk are asleep.

Once upon a time and twice upon a time, there was a little girl, an orphan, who was raised by an old man and an old woman. They lived together in a tiny house made of hemp stalks. It was guarded by the old man's five dogs, named Turpie, Topie, Tippy, Tarry, and Teeny.

The house was at the edge of a great forest. And deep in the woods lived the Hobyahs. They had fur and claws and pointed ears and sharp teeth and tails half again as long as themselves. They slept by day, crept through the woods by night, and plotted against the people in the little hemp-stalk house.

One night,

Silent as the snakes that glide across the forest floor,
Silent as the will-o'-wisps that haunt the reedy shore,
The Hobyahs came....

They wanted to tear down the house of hemp stalks, eat up the old man and woman, and carry off the little girl.

But all the dogs barked, and Turpie barked loudest of all, so the Hobyahs ran off.

The old man said, "Turpie barks so that I cannot sleep nor slumber, and if I live till morning, I will whip him and chase him away."

Though the little girl begged him, "Please don't hurt dear Turpie," the old man whipped the poor animal and ran him off into the forest.

The next night,

Hushed as autumn raindrops patting fallen leaves,
Hushed as fluttered bat wings underneath the eaves,
The Hobyahs came again....

"Hobyah! Hobyah! Hobyah!" they whispered to each other. "Tear down the hemp stalks, eat up the old man and woman, and carry off the little girl!"

But the faithful dog Topie barked so that the Hobyahs ran off.

The old woman complained to her husband, "Topie barks so that I cannot sleep nor slumber. In the morning, you must whip him and chase him away."

The next morning, ignoring the little girl's tears,
the old man chased the dog into the woods.

The following night,

Slyly as a weasel spies a nest through narrowed eyes,
Slyly as a spider sets her snares for careless flies,
The Hobyahs watched and waited....

"Hobyah! Hobyah! Hobyah!" they murmured. "Tear down the hemp stalks, eat up the old man and woman, and carry off the little girl!"

But this time Tippy sounded the alarm, barking and barking until the Hobyahs ran away.

"That wretched Tippy barks so that I cannot sleep nor slumber," said the old man, "and if I live till morning, I will chase him into the woods."

Sure enough, though the little girl begged him to show mercy, the old man would have none of it. He took his whip and chased the faithful hound away.

TETON COUNTY LIBRARY
JACKSON, WYOMING

The next night,

Greedy as the lean red fox that licks her hungry jaws,
Greedy as the owl that flexes his impatient claws,
The Hobyahs came again....

"Hobyah! Hobyah! Hobyah!" they said to one another. "Tear down the hemp stalks, eat up the old man and woman, and carry off the little girl!"

But Tarry barked so loudly that the Hobyahs ran off.

Now the old woman grumbled, "Little dog Tarry barks so much that I cannot sleep nor slumber. Husband, you must get rid of him just as you got rid of the others."

"Please don't hurt dear Tarry," the little girl pleaded, but the grown-ups told her to stand aside. They chased the unhappy hound into the woods with the others.

So, on the following night,

Deadly as the winter snows for those who lose their
*   way,*
Deadly as the hawk that swoops on unsuspecting prey,
The Hobyahs came....

"Hobyah! Hobyah! Hobyah!" they chattered to one another. "Tear down the hemp stalks, eat up the old man and woman, and carry off the little girl!"

But Teeny barked and barked so that the Hobyahs at last ran off.

The old man threw open the shutters and shook his fist at the dog. "You bark so that I cannot sleep nor slumber!" he shouted. "If I live till morning, I will drive you off just like the others."

Sure enough, the very first thing the next
morning, the old man beat the loyal dog and chased
him away.

Now the old man and
woman and the little girl were
all alone in the house
at the edge of the woods.

The next night,

Boldly as the bear whose mighty roaring shakes the
   moon,
Boldly as the wolves that sense the hunt is ending soon,
The Hobyahs came a last time....

"Hobyah! Hobyah! Hobyah!" they cried. "Tear down the hemp stalks, eat up the old man and woman, and carry off the little girl!"

When the Hobyahs found that all five dogs—Turpie, Topie, Tippy, Tarry, and Teeny—were gone, they tore down the hemp-stalk walls, ate up the old man and woman, and carried the little girl off in a bag.

Now, when the Hobyahs came to their home, which was a nasty cave in the heart of the woods, they tossed the bag with the little girl inside it into a corner. Then, because dawn was coming and they slept in the daytime, the Hobyahs all nodded off.

The little girl cried a great deal, because she could not free herself from the bag.

But the faithful dogs that had been chased into the woods heard her crying. They came and chewed a hole in the side of the bag, and the little girl crawled out. Then the five dogs hid in the bag, while the little girl waited outside the Hobyahs' cave.

That night, the Hobyahs woke and gathered around the bag. They knocked on the top of it and cried, "Look me! Look me!"

But when they opened the bag…

Turpie, Topie, Tippy, Tarry, and Teeny jumped out and gobbled them all up. And that was the end of the Hobyahs.

Then the little girl and the five loyal dogs found their way out of the woods. They built a new house of hemp stalks for all of them to share. There they lived contentedly—and if they haven't gone away, they must be living there still.

By moonlight and by starlight,
From dusk until the dawn,
Good folk are sleeping soundly,
With all the Hobyahs gone.

Author's Note

The Hobyahs have intrigued me since I first came across a reference to them in the fascinating Australian film *Celia*. In researching these unfamiliar "bogeys," I discovered that they were actually a bit of transplanted British folklore, which has taken root "down under."

For this retelling, I consulted Joseph Jacobs's version in his classic *More English Folk and Fairy Tales,* published at the turn of the century. Jacobs cites his primary source as a version of the tale gathered in Perth, Scotland, which he found printed in the *Journal of American Folk-Lore.*

I have added the poetry to heighten the sense of setting and menace, and to enhance the story's read-aloud appeal. The major textual change was the substitution of five dogs, run off in sequence, for the original description of a single unhappy "little dog Turpie," who loses tail, legs, and finally head as the story progresses. This change also allowed me to have the dogs rescue the little girl, rather than rely on the unexpected appearance of a hunter and his dog to set things right.

The basis of *The Hobyahs* is probably the traditional European folktale of the faithful watchdog who saves his master's child from a wolf, but is mistakenly accused of harming the child. The dog is put to death before the child he has saved is found safe in hiding.

TETON COUNTY LIBRARY
JACKSON, WYOMING